REBECCA ELSWICK
No Stopping Her

Rebecca D. Elswick is the daughter and grand-daughter of coal miners. She is the director of the Writing Center at the Appalachian School of Law and a consultant for the Appalachian Writing Project at the University of Virginia's college at Wise. Rebecca's work has appeared in many journals and anthologies, such as *A Cup of Comfort for Dog Lovers II, Drafthorse, The Notebook*, and *Broken Petals*. Her short fiction has won many awards, including first place in the Sherwood Anderson Short Story Contest, and she was a finalist for the New Southerner Literary Contest. *Publishers Weekly* praised her debut novel, *Mama's Shoes*, as "an intricate and beautiful landscape...a well-tuned and complex work."

GEMMA
Open Door

First published by GemmaMedia in 2015.

GemmaMedia
230 Commercial Street
Boston MA 02109 USA

www.gemmamedia.com

Printed in the United States of America

978-1-936846-51-1

Library of Congress Cataloging-in-Publication Data

Names: Elswick, Rebecca D.
Title: No stopping her / Rebecca D. Elswick.
Description: Boston MA : GemmaMedia, 2015.
Identifiers: LCCN 2015035224 | ISBN 9781936846511 (softcover)
Subjects: LCSH: Families--Appalachian Region--Fiction. | English
  language--Textbooks for foreign speakers. | Readers (Adult) | Domestic
  fiction.
Classification: LCC PS3605.L79 N6 2015 | DDC 813/.6--dc23 LC
record available at http://lccn.loc.gov/2015035224

Cover by Laura Shaw Design

Inspired by the Irish series designed for new readers, Gemma's Open Doors provide fresh stories, new ideas, and essential resources for young people and adults as they embrace the power of reading and the written word.

Brian Bouldrey
North American Series Editor

GEMMA
Open Door

For Hugh, the love of my life

CHAPTER 1

The word *avarice* floated from the chalkboard, swirled around the room, and became trapped in the dust motes dancing in the sunlight. Brittany Myerson sat with her head propped up by her right hand, pretending to pay attention. Her long blond hair hung next to her chin, hiding her face from the rest of the English class. She was trying to stay awake, she really was, but the teacher's voice sounded like it was coming from far away when it asked, "Can someone give me a definition?"

"*Avarice* means greed," Mason answered.

"Correct."

"Wanting what someone else has like, ah, his car," added Lance.

"Excellent."

Like his car.

The sting of those three words snapped Brittany awake. She knew Lance was throwing that comment at her. She stole a look at him and there it was—that hateful smirk. And then the big jerk winked at her!

Like his car.

Brittany sat up straight and looked at the teacher at the front of the room. She didn't have to turn around to see the sneers on the faces of her classmates. They felt like darts being thrown at her back, each one striking the bull's-eye. Brittany felt heat creep up her neck and flood her face. She stared at the clock, willing the class to be over. This was her last class of the day, and she couldn't wait to get out of there.

When the bell rang, Brittany escaped into the crowded hallway. It was the start of spring break, so she knew everyone would be in a hurry to leave. The hallway cleared fast, making it easy to hang around her locker and wait for the parking lot to empty. After Lance's little stunt, she couldn't deal with the looks and whispers from the drivers in the student parking lot. Besides, she was in no hurry. Facing a week at home made her stomach hurt.

Brittany slammed her locker door shut and looked around for her best friend, Annie. She had hoped Annie had gotten over their argument and decided to ride home with her, but the empty hallway told her that Annie was still mad. Her hateful words rang in Brittany's ears. *Spoiled! Selfish!* She couldn't believe her best friend had called her spoiled and selfish! Annie was supposed to be on her side, but she had gotten mad just because Brittany complained about the crappy car her father had bought for her. Her face flamed remembering Annie's words: "So what if it's not the one you want! At least you *have* a car!"

Not the one I wanted! Oh, no, it's worse than that! Daddy knew I wanted a new VW Bug like the one Lance has, and what did he do?

Hot, angry tears blurred Brittany's vision as she marched out to the parking lot. Her hand shook as she unlocked the door of her used car. It was the ugliest color of yellow she had ever seen in her whole life, and even though it had been cleaned inside and out, the dull gray interior always looked dirty. She had thought, even dreamed, about smashing it into a wall. *Then he would be sorry!*

Brittany tried to pinpoint when her father had begun to change. He had always promised he would buy her a car. For months before she got her driver's license, they had sat together and looked at Volkswagens on the Internet, and not once did he say, "You're not getting a VW Bug." They had discussed convertibles versus sunroofs, leather seats or plush, automatic or manual transmission, and, of course, the color. Black was the only choice, as far as Brittany was concerned. Then last month, Lance Cooper got a new VW Bug for his birthday—a red convertible with black leather seats and tons of extras. He had taken her for a ride and let her babble on about when she would get hers. She had even promised to take him for a ride when she got her new Bug. Brittany felt her face burn with shame just thinking about it.

CHAPTER 2

When Brittany got to the parking lot, it was vacant except for her ugly yellow piece of junk. She unlocked it and slid inside. Her hands clenched the steering wheel. When had it happened? And why had her father changed his mind? She struggled to fit all the pieces together. She remembered her excitement the day she had gotten her driver's license, and how strangely her father had acted. He didn't seem the least bit happy for her, and when she asked if he was going to buy her a car, he had said, "Yes, and if you are old enough to drive, then you are old enough to respect my judgment."

Brittany remembered thinking that it was a strange thing to say, but now his words made sense.

Brittany balled her hands into fists and banged them on the steering wheel. She couldn't believe she had been so clueless! Her father was always spouting out what he called his "words of wisdom." The day she got her license, she had thought he was just doing it again. She remembered smiling at him and saying her usual, "I know, Daddy." She hadn't even realized anything was wrong when he said, "Part of growing up is learning what is important in life. Things that are earned build character."

Stupid! Stupid! Stupid! Brittany rested her forehead on the steering wheel. Her shoulders slumped forward as though a weight had been dropped on her neck. Her father had known she was going to freak out when she saw this hunk of junk on wheels, so he was trying to justify it in advance! He couldn't use money as an excuse. Brittany knew he had the money. He always, *always* bought her what she wanted, but things had changed since he married Lynn. In the past year, her father had slowly turned away from her. It was like he didn't even love her anymore.

Brittany laid her head back against the seat and closed her eyes. She let memories of happier times wash over her. She could see her father, driving her and Annie to the movies, making them laugh with his silly jokes. When the movie was over, he would be waiting in the parking lot to take them for burgers and milkshakes. She thought about their shopping trips together, and how he used to make a big deal about back-to-school shopping. Last year on her birthday, he had bought her the three-hundred-dollar boots she wanted, and every summer they had taken vacations wherever she wanted to go, to places like Disney World and New York City.

Brittany started the car and pulled out of the parking lot. There was one reason why her father had stopped giving her what she asked for—one reason only. It was *her* fault. *She did it! She* made him do it. Anger spread over Brittany like a raging fire. It had been almost a year since her father had married Lynn, and in that year, everything had changed. Now, all their father-daughter talks centered on her need to "grow up," something Lynn had said to her a million times. And Brittany was certain it was Lynn's idea to buy her a used car. That woman had ruined her life.

Brittany remembered the night her father and Lynn announced they were getting married. She pinched her nose together with her fingers and mimicked Lynn's voice. "*I don't ever want to come between you and your father.*"

Brittany took the last turn before her driveway. She could see her house—*her* house! *Not* Lynn's! "You liar!" Brittany screamed. "You lied about everything!"

From the minute they were married, Lynn had set out to turn her father against her. It was Lynn who had talked her father into taking away her credit card and replacing it with a weekly allowance of just twenty dollars. It was her stepmother's idea to supervise her when she went clothes shopping— meaning she refused to buy the designer clothes Brittany wanted, even though *Lynn* wore the same brands. For that matter, she refused to buy anything that Brittany wanted. Instead she tried to get her to wear knockoff brands and department-store crap. When Brittany pointed out that Lynn bought herself expensive clothes, she had dared to say, "When *you* can pay for them yourself, you can buy whatever you want. Until then, I will decide what you can buy."

"We'll see about that," Brittany muttered. She parked her car and got out, leaving the keys in the ignition on purpose. Nothing would make her happier than to come out in the morning and find it gone.

CHAPTER 3

The Saturday her father came home with her car was a day Brittany would never forget. It had started out like any other Saturday. Around noon, she had wandered sleepy-eyed into the empty kitchen and found a note on the table that said, "Be back soon." Since that wasn't unusual, she didn't think anything of it. It did cross her mind that her father could have gone to look at cars, and she thought it would be cool if he surprised her. But she knew he wanted them to pick out her car together—just the two of them. Even if he was going to look at VW's, she couldn't believe he would take her stepmother. But by then, things had changed. Lynn was calling the shots and ruining Brittany's life.

What happened next felt like a nightmare—the kind where no matter how hard you try, you can't wake up. She had replayed it over and over in her mind. It began with her sitting in the kitchen, eating a blueberry muffin and drinking a glass of milk. Next, she heard cars coming up the driveway and honking their horns. She had jumped up and run outside before the cars stopped. The first was a new black VW Bug. The sun bounced off it in waves of spiked white light that almost blinded Brittany. When her father stepped out of the Bug, she had thrown her arms around his neck and danced up and down. She said, "Oh, Daddy, it's perfect! I love it!"

Before her father could say a word, Brittany had jumped into the driver's seat. She inspected the car—her car, or so she thought. She had inhaled that magical new car smell and thought it was the greatest smell in the world. The Bug had everything she wanted: a sunroof, white leather seats, and satellite radio. There was even a small flower vase, and Brittany couldn't wait to buy a tiny rose to put in it.

Brittany recalled looking up at her father and seeing Lynn standing next to him. She had expected to see big smiles on their faces. Instead, her father had his arms folded over his chest, a frown on his face. Her stepmother gave a tight-lipped smirk, as if she had just gotten the last word in an argument. Brittany had looked back down at the car and swept her hand over the steering wheel for what turned out to be the last time. She hopped out and ran over to hug her father again. As she sailed past her stepmother, Brittany could have sworn she heard Lynn snort. Still, she didn't understand what was going on. It wasn't until she tried to wrap her arms back around her father's neck that it happened.

When Brittany's father had stepped back and held up his arm to keep Brittany from hugging him, it got through to her that something was wrong. Still, she thought her father felt bad about them not going together to buy the car. When he said, "Honey, wait a minute. I have to tell you—" Brittany had cut him off and said, "It's okay, Daddy. I know we were going to pick it out together, but surprising me is just as cool!"

It wasn't until her father said, "No, Britt, you don't understand," that she had realized there was another car in the driveway. Behind the shiny new Bug was an ugly two-door junker. It was at least ten years old and an awful yellow color that looked just like baby poop. Brittany remembered feeling like someone had dumped ice water on her body. She had turned away from the cars and looked at her dad, but his face was a stone mask. When she looked at her stepmother, Brittany understood. Lynn had turned her cold gray eyes on Brittany and smiled.

Her father said, "The Bug's not your car."

Not your car.

"Your car is over there."

Not your car.

"Lynn and I thought this would be a perfect first car for you. And later, when you go to college, we can discuss..."

Not your car.

A rush of icy cold wind had roared through Brittany, drowning out his words and leaving her numb. Without looking back, she had walked into the house and up to her room. That day Brittany felt pain so strong she thought she would die from it. All she could do was lie on her bed and rock back and forth saying, "not your car, not your car," over and over. Late that night, she had started to cry. She cried for every day of her life that she had shared with her stepmother. Brittany knew it was all over. Lynn had finally done it. She had taken everything away from her, including her father.

Brittany knew that if she cried and acted out it would give her stepmother more ammunition against her, so the next day she came downstairs for dinner like nothing had happened. Besides, Brittany refused to let her stepmother see her cry. She would not beg for the VW Bug. Even though she seethed with anger on the inside, she acted like the perfect teenager on the outside. She pretended like she was happy with the awful old car that looked the inside of a dirty diaper. Not once did she give her stepmother an excuse to use her favorite argument: "Your father spoils you. It's time you grew up." Brittany even pretended to laugh at the lame joke her father made about the VW Bug. Her ears still rang with his words. "Well, Britt, if your old dad suddenly croaks, the Bug is yours."

And how Lynn had laughed! She had turned her head from side to side, making her gold hoop earrings flash in the light. Then she had stared at Brittany and said, "Oh, no, Bill, it would be *my* car. But of course, I would *give* it to Brittany."

Brittany had stared right back at her stepmother and smiled. She thought, *sure you would*.

CHAPTER 4

Brittany and Annie were friends again, so Brittany drove Annie to and from school. The weather had turned warm and sunny. Gone was the stark black and white of winter. Spring was in full swing. Color had returned to the world, bringing birds and other wildlife in its wake. Soon school would be out, and Brittany and Annie would officially be high school seniors. Everything should have been perfect, but Brittany was miserable.

Annie went out of her way to make Brittany feel better about not getting the car she wanted. She said nice things about the nightmare Brittany's father called a car and bragged on Brittany's driving skills. She thanked Brittany a million times for taking her around, but none of these things made Brittany feel better. In fact, they made her feel worse. Annie was Brittany's best friend, but Annie never let Brittany forget that she had a bigger house and more money than most people, especially her.

Brittany was suffering. She lost weight, she couldn't sleep, and her grades dropped. She could do nothing but think about the day her father had bought two cars—a new VW Bug and a used yellow rust-heap. The only good thing about the situation was that her father was the one driving the Bug. Brittany didn't think she could have stood it if her stepmother had taken the car she had always dreamed of owning. But now, as if things weren't bad enough, Lance and the group of creeps he called friends were tormenting her.

There was no way to avoid Lance. He was one of the most popular kids in school—football star, track star, straight-A student, movie-star handsome. All the teachers loved him because they had no clue that he got his kicks from harassing kids who were not part of his inner circle, or kids like Brittany, who refused to bow down and treat him like royalty.

Lance was a master of the mean, hurtful remark whispered in your ear and the nasty prank that made you look like a fool. And somehow, he never got caught. He was too smart for that. One of the worst things he had ever done was putting a dead cat in Todd Anderson's locker. Poor Todd was an easy target. He was skinny and wore big, thick glasses that made his eyes look like they were floating underwater. Like Lance, he was a straight-A student. Unlike Lance, he was a nerd.

Everybody knew Lance had put the dead cat in Todd's locker because he was furious with Todd for making a higher score on the biology exam. To make matters worse, Todd had dared to brag to everyone that he had beaten Lance. No one was surprised by the prank. Somehow, Lance stole a cat from the biology lab—one of those poor creatures the school bought so students could dissect them. Then, he got Todd's locker combination and put the decaying carcass in the locker, ruining everything in it, including Todd's books, his winter coat, and his backpack.

The principal had spent weeks talking to students, trying to get someone to tell him who did it, but no one ever breathed a word. No one was brave enough to point the finger at Lance. Finally, the principal gave up. Just like every other dirty rotten trick he had done in the past, Lance got away with it.

CHAPTER 5

Now Lance was tormenting Brittany. Yesterday, she and Annie had been eating lunch in the cafeteria when he walked up to Brittany and said, "Hey, Britt, do you want some *mustard* to go with your sandwich?" He had even dropped a packet of mustard on her tray and said, "We all know how much you love that yellow *mustard*. You love it so much, you bought a *mustard*-colored car!"

The noise in the cafeteria died like somebody had thrown an off switch. Everyone turned and looked at Brittany, waiting to see what she would do. She had done nothing. She had simply watched Lance and his group of friends walk away, laughing at her. Lance and his girlfriend had even high-fived each other. Brittany pretended it didn't matter, but she had seen the looks she got from the people sitting around her. Annie had fumed and fussed, but she knew there was nothing Brittany could do but hope that somebody else would come along whom Lance would rather torment.

Two days later, Brittany opened her locker and found a huge jar of mustard on top of her books. It was one of those gallon containers with the words yellow mustard in big block letters on it. The jar was open, but none of it had been spilled on her stuff. She knew she was lucky Lance hadn't poured it all over her books. Still, her whole locker smelled like mustard. Brittany swung around, and there was Lance and his crew, watching her. Lance was doubled over laughing. As much as Brittany wanted to pick up the mustard and throw it at him, she knew that if she did, she would be the one to get into trouble. She just slammed the door shut and stalked off to history class without her book.

After school, Brittany waited for everyone to leave. Then she and Annie got a trash bag and put the mustard in it, wrapping it up before throwing it in the trash can. Annie was furious, but even she knew there was nothing Brittany could do except wait for Lance to get tired of making fun of her. After that day, Brittany started carrying all her books around in a book bag in case he decided to attack. She knew that if he did, it would be much worse.

Brittany did everything she could to avoid Lance and his friends, and for a few days they left her alone. Then she ran right into them. It was the one of those rare days when Annie didn't ride home with her, so she was by herself when she rounded the corner and saw Lance and his friends standing in the student parking lot. "Great, just great," she said. "I have to walk right past them."

Brittany clutched the strap of her book bag and walked faster. She held her car keys in her hand so she could jump in the car and take off, but she didn't make it. Lance spotted her.

"Hey, Britt!" Lance started toward her, his friends following close on his heels. "Where are you going in such a hurry?"

She put her head down and kept walking, but Lance didn't give up. He walked over to her car and leaned against it, crossing one ankle over the other and putting his hand on the hood. His girlfriend came over and stood next to him. The rest of his group crowded around the car.

Brittany was surrounded. She stopped and shouted, "What do you want?"

Lance smiled. "I just want to ask you a question."

"What?" Brittany asked. She heard her voice shake and bit her lip.

Lance said, "I just want to know when you're getting your Volkswagen." He smiled and stretched his arm around his girlfriend's shoulders. "What was it you said?" He put his other hand up to his forehead and tapped it with his forefinger like he was trying to remember.

His girlfriend giggled, and Lance said, "Oh, I remember! You said you were getting a black VW Bug. Right?"

Brittany looked first at Lance, then glanced at the group of Lance wannabes standing around her car. All of them sneered at her, waiting to see what she was going to say. She blinked back hot tears but said nothing.

Lance said, "Oh, yeah, that's right. You didn't get a Bug, you got this little number." He patted the hood of her car. "You got this *mustard*-colored piece of crap, instead. Good choice, Britt."

Lance's friends burst out laughing. Brittany tried to speak loud and clear, but her voice shook when she said, "Ha, ha, very funny. Now will you get away from my car? I'm late."

Lance raised up his arms and shrugged. He smiled at her and said, "Let's go, guys. Brittany has to go buy some more *mustard*."

Brittany got into her car and slammed the door. She glanced in the rearview mirror to make sure Lance and his creeps were leaving. Their laughter rang in her ears, and the tears she had been holding back poured down her cheeks.

"Why?" she cried out loud, pounding her fists on the steering wheel. "Why are you doing this to me?"

Brittany started the car and pulled out of the parking lot. This was all *her* fault! None of this would be happening if her stepmother hadn't ruined her life. The tears fell faster, and Brittany couldn't see the road. She pulled off and put the car in park. She laid her head against the steering wheel and cried until she couldn't cry anymore. When her tears were spent, Brittany made a decision. "*You* will pay," she said. "If it takes me the rest of my life, *you will pay* for what you've done to me." She pulled back onto the road and drove home. It was time to do something about her stepmother.

CHAPTER 6

A month passed. Brittany and Annie were sitting on the floor in Brittany's bedroom laughing at the freshmen's pictures in the yearbook. School was out next week and the summer stretched before them. Annie interrupted Brittany's giggles by standing up and announcing, "Hey, let's go down to the mall and apply for a job at the theater. I hear they're hiring."

"No, thanks," Brittany answered, avoiding Annie's eyes.

"Why not?"

Brittany turned a page in the yearbook. She mumbled, "I've already got a job for the summer."

"What! Why didn't you tell me?"

Brittany snapped her book shut and stood up. "I'm going to do the summer job-shadowing program at the Pet Vet Clinic where Lynn works."

Annie stared at her like she had snakes crawling out of her ears. She said, "Have you lost your mind? I thought you hated your stepmother, and now you're telling me you want to spend your summer following her around!"

Brittany put her hands on her hips and announced, "I'm exploring the field of veterinary medicine. Maybe I'll follow in Lynn's footsteps."

Annie wasn't buying it. "And maybe I'll go to England and meet the queen."

There were two things Brittany knew

she could count on where Annie was concerned. One, she would rather hear gossip than eat chocolate fudge. Two, she couldn't keep a secret if her life depended on it. Brittany turned around and crossed the room to her open door. She glanced out into the hall before shutting the door. When she turned around she spoke softly. "Annie, I have a very good reason for working at my stepmother's clinic. I need to keep an eye on her."

Eyes wide, Annie breathed, "Why?"

"I have my reasons. *Good* reasons. That's all I can say right now."

CHAPTER 7

Bright and early on the first day of summer vacation, Brittany drove to work at her stepmother's veterinary clinic. She pitched right in, tackling any task, no matter how boring or unpleasant. She cleaned out animal cages, changed food and water containers, and took out the trash. She even volunteered to stock the shelves, stacking heavy bags of dog food.

At first, Lynn treated Brittany like the maid. She constantly gave Brittany cleaning jobs to do. She even invented things for Brittany to clean. Brittany knew Lynn was trying to make her quit, so the more awful the jobs, the more cheerful and upbeat she acted. After two weeks, Lynn told Brittany's father that Brittany was "doing a good job." By midsummer, Lynn was happy that Brittany was working for her. She even started asking for Brittany when she needed help with an animal.

One day, Lynn gave Brittany a couple of books on veterinary medicine. That night at dinner, Brittany proudly showed them to her father.

He said, "Well, Britt, are you thinking about vet school?"

"Yes, Daddy. What do you think?"

Instead of smiling like Brittany had expected, her father just looked relieved. Before Brittany could say another word, Lynn spoke up. "She does show some potential, but she's going to have to dedicate her senior year to taking math and science classes. Of course, she'll need two years at the community college before she will be ready for university study."

Brittany was too stunned to speak. She looked at her father, but he wouldn't look at her. Instead, he smiled at Lynn and nodded. Brittany couldn't believe it! Her stepmother was staring at her with her cool gray eyes. Brittany swallowed and tried to calm herself. She didn't want her voice to shake, or worse, to sound like a little girl pleading to get her way. She leaned toward her father, hoping he could see the pained look in her eyes and said, "Daddy, I want to go north to college like my mother did. You know that."

Brittany could see the redness creeping up his neck, a sure sign he was upset. He looked down at his plate and acted like he was busy cutting his roast. He said, "We have a while yet to discuss what college is best for you."

Brittany said, "But Daddy, you know I'm planning to apply for early admission." She stopped. Panic paralyzed her diaphragm. She was afraid she was going to throw up.

Then Lynn said, "Britt, your father knows what's best for you. There's a perfectly good community college just down the road from here, and remember, you do have your own *car*."

Brittany felt a scream rising up inside her, threatening to tear her apart. She wanted to end the perfect teenager game and throw a fit, but she held on. She took a deep breath and sat very still. *Community college? She wants to send me to a community college?* She wouldn't look at Lynn. Instead, she turned pleading eyes on her father, but he was looking up at Lynn like she was the most beautiful and intelligent woman in the world.

Her father finally said, "Of course you can apply. In fact, you should apply to several colleges. Then we can discuss your options as your senior year progresses." His eyes shifted to Lynn, and he smiled. "But Lynn's right. No matter what you decide to study, the community college is a good idea, and if you're interested in veterinary medicine, then Lynn can certainly advise you."

Lynn said, "Honey, don't let Brittany upset you. Remember what the doctor said about your blood pressure and your heart."

Brittany watched her father reach for Lynn's hand. He kissed it and said, "Now, don't you worry about me. I'm taking my medicine." Then he turned and looked at Brittany. The cold stillness of his blue eyes shocked her. He said, "Brittany isn't going to upset me. Are you, Brittany?"

Brittany slowly shook her head no. It was all over. There was no room for Brittany in his life anymore. She was sure of that now. Brittany turned and looked at her stepmother. Lynn's smoky gray eyes looked like cold, hard steel. She flashed Brittany a smile. Brittany had seen that smile many times. It was the same smile she used on people at the vet clinic when she wanted to get rid of them. Lynn said, "Brittany, we both want what's best for you."

The phone rang. Brittany excused herself and went to answer it in the kitchen. Annie had a knack for calling at just the right time.

CHAPTER 8

With summer vacation speeding toward an end, Brittany found the veterinary assistants relying on her more and more. When her stepmother and father went to Hawaii on vacation, Brittany worked every day at the clinic. She even volunteered to do the stock inventory, and she made sure the office manager saw her report. Then it was time to stop dropping hints and let Annie know what her stepmother was up to.

With Lynn and her father safely in Hawaii, Brittany took Annie into her father's study. She handed her a folder full of papers and told her to sit down and start reading. Brittany sat next to Annie and waited. All of a sudden, Annie started shaking the papers like they had caught on fire.

Annie said, "This is bad. This is really bad!"

Brittany said, "I told you I needed to stay close to her this summer."

Annie spread the papers out on the desk. Brittany came over to stand next to her. She knew Annie loved investigating things. She was like a dog with a bone until she figured it out.

Brittany said, "This house belonged to my mother's family. It was supposed to be mine someday. My father told me that he promised my mother before she died that it would go to me." Brittany picked up one of the papers and handed it to Annie. She said, "Look at this. It's called a codicil. I looked it up on the Internet. It means that the old will, which gave me all of Dad's estate, is null and void."

"Null and void. You mean, like, it doesn't count anymore?" Annie asked.

"That's exactly what it means," Brittany said.

Annie said, "All of it? Are you sure he gave her all of it?"

"Read this," Brittany said, pointing to a paragraph. "It says here that all other wills are null and void, and that he leaves all of his estate to his wife, Lynn. That means the only thing I get is the trust fund my mother left me, and that's just because she can't touch it."

Brittany opened her father's desk and took out another folder. She opened it, pulled out a paper, and handed it to Annie. "Look at this. It's a new life insurance policy on my dad for half a million dollars. And guess who the primary beneficiary is?"

Annie sat down in her father's desk chair. She looked up at Brittany. "Your dad has made Lynn the primary beneficiary and you the secondary beneficiary on everything. That means if something happens to him, Lynn will get everything because she is the primary, and the only way you will get anything is if something happens to her."

Brittany nodded her head yes. A tear slipped down her cheek. Annie sprang up and put her arm around her friend.

She said, "Brittany, don't cry. Your dad changed this once. He can change it again."

Brittany whispered. "Not if he dies first."

"Hey," Annie said. "Your dad's not going to die." She gently pushed Brittany away so she could look into her eyes. "He's going to live a long, long time."

"No, Annie. He has high blood pressure and high cholesterol and the doctor told him he needs to stop drinking and exercise." Brittany started pacing back and forth. She said, "Don't you see, Lynn's a lot younger than him, and she's gotten him to sign everything over to her."

"What are you saying?"

"I'm saying," Brittany said, stopping right in front of Annie, "I don't trust her.

I never have. Think about it. She loves to travel. She spends thousands of dollars on expensive clothes and jewelry. And—"

Annie interrupted, "And she doesn't want your father to spend any money on you—used car, community college."

"Exactly," Brittany said.

Brittany and Annie sat down on the floor. Annie said, "I see what you mean. But you don't think she would, well, kill your father? Do you?"

"I don't know."

The tone of Brittany's voice must have gotten through to her, because Annie's face paled. Brittany said, "Think about it, Annie. I'll be eighteen soon and out of high school. If my dad dies, she'll take everything." Brittany stood up and started putting everything back in her father's desk. She arranged thing just as he had, so no one would suspect she had touched anything. Brittany knew she had to be careful. If there was one thing she had learned this summer, it was that her stepmother was incredibly smart.

Annie grabbed Brittany by the shoulders and turned her around to face her. Her eyes were wide and her face was pale. Slowly and deliberately she said, "Brittany, you have to tell somebody."

"No!" Brittany took Annie's face in her hands. She looked deeply into her friend's eyes. "Nobody can know about this but you. You have to swear you won't tell. Not now."

CHAPTER 9

School began, and Brittany started marking off the days until her eighteenth birthday. The best part about being a senior was that Lance wasn't in any of her classes. She and Annie even had a different lunch period than he did, so she barely saw him.

Just as she had planned, Brittany applied to her mother's alma mater, Wellesley College in Massachusetts. Right before the holidays, she found out she had been accepted. Brittany couldn't stop thinking about her mother. Sometimes a flash of color or a scent on the air would make her think of her. She knew so little about her that she wasn't sure if her memories were real or imagined.

Her father never wanted to talk about her mother. He had told Brittany that her mother died in a car accident when she was five. Brittany had been in the car and escaped without major injuries, but that was all she knew about the accident. When she was twelve, she had asked her father so many questions that he finally gave her a keepsake box that had belonged to her mother. He seemed to think that would satisfy Brittany's curiosity.

The box itself was beautiful. It was a big, round, old hatbox. It was covered in a silky material that had once been a dark rose, but it had faded to a soft pink. The top of the box had a twisted rope of black leather that made a handle, so the box was easy to carry. That box held her mother's memories, and it was Brittany's most prized possession. She had pored over the photo albums filled with pictures of her mother with her friends. She cherished the scrapbooks filled with birthday cards, movie tickets, pieces of ribbon, letters and notes from friends, and crushed flowers that Brittany imagined had been given to her by boyfriends.

Brittany's favorite scrapbook was the one filled with Wellesley College memorabilia. Inside its leather cover were ticket stubs from football games, programs from college plays and orchestras, more dried flowers, and corsage ribbons with the pearl-topped stickpins still attached. Most precious to Brittany was a pair of white gloves. Brittany had put them on her hands thousands of times and imagined her mother dressed in a sparkling white ball gown, wearing the same gloves. Every keepsake of her mother's said she had loved this college. When Brittany was twelve years old, she had decided she would go to Wellesley College. *No one* was going to stop her. Not her stepmother. Not her father.

Brittany waited until she was sure her stepmother wasn't home before she showed her father the acceptance letter from Wellesley College. She watched him read it and saw his throat begin to flush. Before he could say a word, she started begging him to let her go. She even laid her mother's scrapbook on the table in front of him. He slowly turned each page, and when he was finished, he closed the book and handed it back to Brittany. All he would say was, "I'll think about it."

Brittany exploded. She yelled, "Think about it! You'll think about it! What's that supposed to mean?"

"It means exactly what I said. You don't have to decide right now. I'll talk to Lynn and we can—"

Brittany screamed, "Talk to Lynn! You'll talk to Lynn? Lynn is not my mother!" She balled her hands into fists and said, "She has no right to say anything about what I do with my life!"

Her father's face turned white. He sat up and glared at Brittany. He said, "Lynn is part of this family, and she certainly does have a say in all decisions. She, she..." He stopped talking and clutched his chest. He said, "Get my pills. They're in my bedroom on my nightstand."

Brittany ran upstairs and found the container of pills. She hurried back down and grabbed a bottle of water out of the refrigerator before taking it and the pills to her father. She sat down next to him and said, "Daddy, I'm so sorry I yelled at you."

He took a pill and drank some water. Then he put his hand on Brittany's knee. He said, "I'm okay. I just need to rest. I think I'll stretch out on the couch a minute."

Brittany stood up and kissed him on the cheek. She picked up the bottle of pills and said, "I'm going upstairs. I'll put these back for you."

When Brittany returned the pills to her father's nightstand, she took one and hid it in her jewelry box. She wanted to remember what it looked like.

CHAPTER 10

In January, Brittany came home from school and found her father lying on the couch, covered with a blanket. She asked, "What's wrong, Daddy?"

"I'm just a little tired," he said.

"Well, I have something to make you feel better," Brittany said. She handed him her midterm grades.

He looked at the paper and smiled. "I'm proud of you, Brittany," he said. "You got all A's."

"Thanks, Daddy. So, I can go to Wellesley, right?"

He handed the grades back to her and said, "No, Brittany. You need to stay here for the first year and go to the community college."

Brittany dropped down on her knees next to her father. "Daddy, please, I've gotten all A's!" She laid her head on his chest and sobbed.

When she looked up, her father's face was red, but he stared at her with eyes as cold as steel. He said, "I've made my decision."

Annie had come home with Brittany after school, but she had waited in the kitchen while Brittany talked to her father. She heard the argument loud and clear. It didn't take her long to figure out that he had told Brittany she couldn't go to Wellesley. When Annie heard her running up the stairs, she knew Brittany was going to her room. She didn't want to walk by Brittany's father, who was still in the living room. Instead, she went up the narrow kitchen stairs. These stairs also went to the second floor, but came out at the back of the house. Annie found her friend on her bed, crying like her heart was breaking. She tried to calm her down, but Brittany cried for an hour. All she could say between sobs was, "It's over. It's over."

Brittany begged Annie to stay for dinner so she wouldn't have to face her stepmother and father alone. Annie agreed, and she did most of the talking during the meal. Poor Annie tried to act like it was just a typical day—like her best friend hadn't just had her hopes and dreams destroyed. When dinner was over, Annie breathed a sigh of relief.

She offered to help with the dishes, but Lynn waved her away and told the girls she was sure they needed to do homework.

They went to Brittany's room and closed the door. Annie said, "Brittany, your dad doesn't look so good."

"I know," Brittany said. "I think my stepmother is giving him something."

Annie's eyes went wide. "Like what?"

Brittany said, "Every night after dinner, my stepmother puts my dad's medicine in this little pill container. She divides them into his morning pills and his nighttime pills, and she makes sure he takes them."

Annie said, "Can't he do that himself?"

"That's just it," Brittany said. "She

won't *let* him do it. She tries to make a joke about it. She says she has to do it or he might forget, but I think she's giving him the wrong medicine on purpose."

Annie said, "Oh, god, Brittany. You have to tell somebody!"

"Listen, Annie, I have to be sure. I can't just accuse my stepmother of trying to kill my father without proof."

Annie sat down on the bed. "You're right," she said. "But how are you going to get proof?"

"I'm working on it. You just have to let me handle it."

Annie nodded her head. "I understand, but it wouldn't hurt to tell somebody that you were worried about your dad, and—"

"And what? That my stepmother is

killing him?" Brittany said. "The first thing they'd do is call my father, or worse, my stepmother."

Annie sighed. "I see what you mean."

Brittany jumped up and grabbed Annie by the hand. "Let's go downstairs and act like we're getting something to drink."

"Why?" Annie asked.

"Because that way we can see what Lynn's doing."

Brittany and Annie walked into the kitchen and found Lynn sitting at the table with bottles of pills and a pillbox in front of her. She jerked her head up and pressed her hand to her chest. She gasped. "Girls, you scared me!"

Brittany mumbled, "Sorry," and opened the refrigerator.

"What are you doing, Mrs. Myerson?" Annie asked. Her voice was sweet and innocent like she was asking about the weather. Brittany had her head inside the refrigerator, so she knew her stepmother couldn't see her when she smiled.

Brittany grabbed two Cokes. She knew Annie like the back of her hand, so she acted busy getting glasses and ice while Annie talked to her stepmother. She also knew that Lynn put her father's pills out every night after dinner. She had timed this little visit to the kitchen so they would catch her at it. She wanted Annie to see for herself how her stepmother handled all her father's medicine.

Lynn said, "I'm just making sure Brittany's dad takes the right medicine."

"Oh, yeah?" Annie said.

"Yes, it's very important that he take the right medicine at the right time. He has a bad heart, you know."

Brittany turned around and handed Annie a Coke. Annie said, "Well, what would happen if he didn't take his medicine? Would he get sick?"

Lynn snapped the lid down on the pillbox and stood up. She looked at Brittany and said, "It could be fatal. Isn't that right, Brittany?"

Brittany nodded her head yes and grabbed Annie's arm. She said, "Let's go finish our homework."

When the girls got back upstairs, Brittany started crying. Annie put her arm around her friend and tried to comfort her. Annie said, "I saw it with my own eyes. I saw her with your dad's medicine. She could've been putting anything in that pillbox."

"That's right," Brittany said. "From here on out I'm going to watch every move she makes, and if my dad starts acting like he's having a heart attack, I'm calling the doctor myself."

CHAPTER 11

A week later, a snowstorm hit, and the power was out for two days. Brittany was trapped in the family room with her father and stepmother because that room had a gas-powered fireplace. Brittany slept in the recliner and watched her stepmother fuss over her father. When the power finally came back on, they celebrated with hot chocolate and a game of cards. Brittany's father had developed a cough and Lynn begged him to go to the doctor, but he waved it off, saying he felt fine.

Lynn was able to go to work the next day. Schools were still closed, though, so it was just Brittany and her father. Brittany decided she would ask one last time if he would change his mind and let her go to Wellesley.

She had just started to steer the conversation toward college when her father stopped her. "There's no use," he said. "I haven't changed my mind. Lynn was right. There's absolutely no reason to waste money at an expensive college when you can get the same classes right here at home."

Brittany blinked back the tears that stung her eyes.

"Daddy, please," she begged.

"I may as well tell you that Lynn and I are thinking about selling the house. This old house is too much for Lynn, with her work at the clinic. She's been looking at some town houses. They have all the modern conveniences. Of course, you would have your own room."

"But Daddy, this was my mother's house!" Tears ran freely down Brittany's face. "This is supposed to be *my* house someday."

Her father stared at her. His face was white, and the red was creeping up his neck. He said, "I don't understand you. You were only five when she died. You can barely remember her. It's time you stopped all this nonsense about your mother. It's time you listened to Lynn and me."

He reached for the bottle of pills he took when he was upset. Brittany knew these were supposed to bring down his blood pressure and heart rate. She stood and steadied herself. She wiped the tears from her face, walked over, and picked up the bottle. "Here Daddy, let me get your medication for you," she said. She opened the bottle and shook two pills into his outstretched hand.

"Call 911! Brittany, call 911! Your father's not breathing!"

A blur of flashing lights, the scream of sirens, and the icy cold air hit Brittany as she ran out the door to meet the ambulance. Up and down the street, the neighbors were coming outside to stand in their front yards and watch what was happening. The Watsons, who lived across the street, came running to Brittany. Mrs. Watson reached her first. "What happened?

How can we help?"

Brittany threw herself into Mrs. Watson's arms. "It's my daddy! He's not breathing!"

Mr. and Mrs. Watson held Brittany back while the paramedics rushed into the house. She sobbed on Mrs. Watson's shoulder and kept saying, "Daddy," over and over. When the paramedics wheeled the stretcher back out of the house, Brittany tried to run to the ambulance, but her legs gave way. If Mr. Watson hadn't caught her, she would have fallen on the ground. When her stepmother disappeared inside the ambulance with her father, Brittany buried her face in her hands so the Watsons and the neighbors, who had gathered around to comfort her, wouldn't see her face.

CHAPTER 12

Brittany graduated from high school a week before her stepmother went on trial for her father's murder. She sat in the courtroom between her best friend, Annie, and her high school guidance counselor, Miss Williams. As the terrible murder plot unfolded, at times Brittany looked amazed, and at other times, she cried softly.

The day Brittany watched the police arrest her stepmother had been one of the happiest of her life. Since her father's funeral, she had refused to live in the house with Lynn, and instead stayed across the street with Mr. and

Mrs. Watson. It was Mr. Watson who had first seen the police car. By the time the police dragged Lynn out of the house kicking and screaming, Brittany and the Watsons were standing in the yard watching Lynn get arrested. Brittany shivered when she heard the police officer say, "Lynn Myerson, you are under arrest for the murder of your husband, William Myerson. You have the right to remain silent..."

On the first day of the trial, the prosecuting attorney told the court he would prove that Lynn Myerson had planned and carried out a horrible plot to kill her husband, William. He told the jury that Lynn had first switched her husband's heart medication for a look-alike over-the-counter diet pill that raised his blood pressure and made his heart beat faster. Second, the attorney called witnesses who said that Lynn had told them she was afraid her husband was going to have a heart attack. Third, the attorney called a special witness who was a veterinarian and a medical doctor. He testified that a veterinarian who knew how much barbiturate to give an animal to stop its heart would also know how much to give a human to make it look like a fatal heart attack.

The prosecuting attorney pointed out that the one thing Lynn hadn't counted on was that Brittany would find her father's new will and insurance policy and tell her friend Annie. Even though Brittany was too scared to tell an adult about it, Annie had confided everything

Brittany told her to the school's guidance counselor, Miss Williams.

As the trial wore on, the evidence mounted against Lynn. When the police searched the house, they found a syringe and needle hidden in a toothbrush holder in the guest bathroom. It contained traces of the same barbiturate that had killed Brittany's father, and it had Lynn's fingerprints on it. The prosecutor called it the murder weapon. He said that Lynn had used it to inject the drug into her husband on the night he died.

The most damaging testimony of all came from Lynn's office manager, who swore under oath that when Brittany worked at her stepmother's vet clinic, she had done an inventory showing that barbiturates were missing. The prosecution produced the inventory sheet, including a handwritten note from Brittany that asked her stepmother to recheck the stock of barbiturates. The office manager said she had verified Brittany's inventory and had also asked Dr. Myerson to check for the missing stock. Dr. Myerson had told her she would take care of it.

CHAPTER 13

Lynn took the witness stand in her own defense. Brittany came to court dressed in a black skirt and sweater, knee socks, and plain black shoes. She wore no makeup and pulled her hair into a ponytail. She looked much younger than eighteen, and she was happy with the effect. Still, it was the picture of her father that had the greatest impact. Brittany brought a framed picture of her father and sat with it on her lap.

From the minute the prosecutor started questioning Lynn, she began to fall apart. By the time the prosecutor asked, "Did you kill your husband,

Bill Myerson?" Lynn was crying uncontrollably. The audience could barely hear her say, "No, I did not."

What happened next would remain with Brittany for the rest of her life. She would play it over and over again in her mind, and each time it got better and better. The prosecutor slowly walked away from Lynn and stopped in front of the jury. With his back to Lynn, he faced the jury and said, "If you didn't kill Bill Myerson, then who did?"

Brittany stared at her stepmother, who shifted her gaze from the prosecutor's back to Brittany's face. That's when Brittany smiled—just the slightest smile—but her stepmother saw it. She pointed her finger at Brittany and screamed, "She did it! Brittany did it!

She killed her father!"

The court room erupted like a volcano, and everyone started talking at once. Officers grabbed Lynn, who was trying to crawl out of the witness box while still screaming at Brittany. The judge banged his gavel and yelled, "Order! Order in the court!" And through it all, Brittany held her father's picture in her arms and cried softly while her best friend, Annie, tried to comfort her.

EPILOGUE

The jury found Lynn Myerson guilty. By the time summer was over, Lynn was behind bars for good and Brittany was packing her things for Wellesley College. Her dream was coming true after all. She was going to the same college her mother had attended, just like she had always wanted.

A lawyer took care of everything, and Brittany Myerson inherited the house, all the insurance money, and all her father's assets and possessions, including the black Volkswagen. She gave the yellow car to Annie.

When everything was packed,

Brittany locked up *her* house, climbed into *her* black VW Bug, and backed out of *her* driveway. Without looking back, she headed for Massachusetts to the college of *her* choice where she would begin *her* new life.

The Ugly Duckling
A Tale of Patience

The Ugly Duckling
A Tale of Patience

Illustrated by Susan Spellman

Other illustrations by Marty Noble

Adapted by Sarah Toast

Publications International, Ltd.

Once upon a time, on a lovely spring day in the country, something exciting was about to happen. A mother duck was sitting on her nest by the edge of a pond. She had been waiting a very long time for her eggs to hatch. It seemed like she had been sitting there forever!

Finally the eggs began to crack. "Peep, peep," said the newly hatched ducklings.

"Quack, quack," said their mother. "You are the sweetest little yellow ducklings I have ever seen! Are you all here?" She stood up to look in the nest. She saw that the biggest egg hadn't hatched yet.

The tired mother duck sat down again on the last egg. When it finally cracked open, out tumbled a clumsy, gray baby bird. He was bigger than the others, and he didn't look like them. In fact, he was rather funny looking.

"Peep, peep," said the big baby. The mother duck looked at him. "He's awfully big for his age," she thought to herself. "I wonder if he can swim?"

The next day, the sun shone brightly. The mother duck led her ducklings to the pond. "Quack, quack," she told them, and the ducklings understood. One after the other, the eager little ducklings jumped into the water. They bobbed and floated like little corks. They knew how to paddle their legs and swim without being told.

All of the new baby birds swam very nicely, even the one who looked different. "He may have too long a neck," thought the mother duck, "but see how nicely he holds it. If you tilt your head a little bit, he almost looks handsome." The baby ducklings practiced their swimming the rest of the afternoon.

The mother duck was very pleased. All her ducklings swam well, especially the gray one.

The mother duck decided it was time to take her babies to the farm to meet the other ducks. "Quack, quack," she said. "Follow me! Keep your legs far apart. Waddle like this."

The gray duckling could not quite get it right. The other baby ducks on the farm gathered around him and said, "Look how ugly that duckling is!" One big duck came over and quacked, "Stay out of my way, you ugly duckling!"

"Leave him alone!" cried the mother duck. "He may not be good-looking, but he is kind and he can swim as well as anyone—maybe better!" No one listened to her. The other ducks acted mean and chased the poor ugly duckling.

A few days later, the other ducklings were playing on the farm. They wouldn't let the ugly duckling join in any of the games. For a while, the little duckling sat all alone. Then he got an idea that made him smile. "I'll practice my swimming!" he said to himself.

The ugly duckling went to the pond and swam and swam and swam. When he stopped, he was very tired. Then he looked around. He was lost!

What was that noise? A big hunting dog was very close! The ugly duckling hid in the tall grass. He was so afraid to move that he stayed in the water all night.

When morning came, the ugly duckling was sure the dog had gone. The baby duck was still lost. But now he was also hungry, and even a little scared. The poor duckling knew he had to do something.

"I'll just have to try to find something to eat," said the ugly duckling. He hopped out of the pond and looked around. There was a farm down the road. He waddled closer to take a look. Near the farmhouse he saw a woman. "Peep," said the duckling.

The woman said, "You look hungry. Come into my house and have something to eat." As soon as they arrived in the kitchen, the ugly duckling saw a cat and a pet hen. The cat and hen stared right at the ugly duckling. The duckling stared at the floor.

The duckling couldn't lay eggs like the hen or purr like the cat. They picked on him because he was different. After a few days, the duckling remembered how much he liked to be in the fresh air and how much he missed swimming in the water. One night he quietly left the house.

The duckling waddled farther down the road. He found a lake filled with wild ducks where he stayed for many weeks. The duckling could dive to the bottom of the lake and pop up again. The swimming helped him grow bigger and stronger. Still, none of the wild ducks would talk to him because they thought he was too ugly.

Soon autumn arrived. The leaves turned colors, and the air got cooler. The water became cooler, too. One evening, just at sunset, a flock of beautiful birds flew over the lake. Their feathers were shiny white, and they had long, graceful necks. The birds were flying south to find a warmer place to live for the winter.

The ugly duckling stretched his neck to look at the beautiful birds. He felt sad as he watched them fly away. Soon he was shivering, and he felt very lonely.

Winter came, and the pond turned to ice. A duck cannot swim on ice. The ugly duckling needed to practice, so he went in search of water that wasn't frozen.

Soon he came to a farmhouse. It looked very warm and cozy. There was a fireplace with a roaring fire in it. The ugly duckling waddled into the house and began his search. Finally he found something. It was much smaller than the pond, but it would just have to do. He jumped in and started to swim.

The farmer's wife heard a lot of splashing. She was very surprised to find a large bird inside the house! She quickly grabbed the broom and chased him back out into the snow, knocking over a fresh bucket of milk in the process. The children laughed and laughed at the big bird who had tried to swim in their bathtub.

The duckling was very scared! He found a hiding place under some bushes. Snow fell all around him. He tried to stay warm.

The ugly duckling had a hard time that long winter. There was barely any food to eat, and the icy wind made him very cold.

Just when the duckling thought winter would never end, spring arrived! Now there was warm sunshine and blooming flowers. Many birds came back from their winter homes.

It was now warm enough to go back on the lake. How good it felt to swim on the water again. He stretched his neck all around. When he looked down, what a surprise he got!

There in the water he saw the most beautiful bird. He looked at the swans swimming farther down the lake. They must know this swan below the water.

The ugly duckling was surprised when he heard someone speak to him. "Come join us," the swans said. What? Could this be true? Could the beautiful swans really be talking to him?

The ugly duckling looked down in the water again. Why, that wasn't another bird at all. It was his own reflection that he saw in the water. Over the winter, the ugly duckling had grown into a beautiful swan. He really wasn't a duck at all. No wonder he didn't fit in.

The other swans circled around him and stroked him with their beaks. All the young swan had gone through made him appreciate his newfound happiness. He saw beauty in all that surrounded him. He ruffled his feathers and thought, "I never dreamed I could be so happy when I was an ugly duckling."

One to Grow On
Patience

Almost everyone was mean to the ugly duckling. They called him names and made fun of him. Do you think this made him feel good?

Sometimes it is hard to be patient with others who are different from us. Do you think things would be easier if everyone was the same?

Different people have different ways of seeing things. We can learn important lessons by talking and listening to people who are different from us. And remember, today's ugly duckling can be tomorrow's beautiful swan.

The End